The Widower Of Darkness 2

Companion Of Darkness

M.Y. Hauger

Introduction

After the disappearance of Aston's son, Hayden, Steve advised the young man to take his family and go to the underground shelter where they would be safe. They agreed that it would be in the best interest of the family if they would be kept hidden, especially in light of everything that had happened during that time. Aston also wanted Steve and his family to stay in the underground shelter with him and his family. Without hesitation, Steve agreed to it because he wanted to see to it that the family remained safe.

During that time, Endymion, who was Aston's father, came to the family during the night. He often brought food and other things that they would need. He also spent time with his remaining grandson, Hugh, whenever he was able to.

No one else was aware of the fact that Aston was keeping his family hidden. He went about his life, doing the things he normally did, and no one suspected a thing. Now and then, Levi would ask Aston about Hugh because he had not seen him around. Aston would either pretend that he didn't hear him or he'd simply tell him that he's doing fine, and then he'd walk away. Sometimes, Steve would glare at Levi as he shook his fist at him, letting him know that he knew what he was up to. Levi would just roll his eyes, shake his head, and then walk away.

While the men were at work, Rose and Jasmine took care of the things that needed to be done in the shelter. They also worked together to take care of the children, who bonded with one another over time. Hugh remained quiet, even as he played with Steve's children, who didn't seem to mind. They also wanted to cheer Hugh up because they knew that he was sad because his brother was missing. Hugh missed his twin brother, and he wished that he was there with them. Even though he was sad about his brother not being there, he was thankful that he was no longer being tormented by Levi. During that time, it seemed that the boy had managed to find peace as he remained hidden in the underground shelter.

Chapter 1

The people of the community continued to blame Endymion for the disappearance of Hayden, but the truth was, he was innocent. It was Delano who had taken the child, not leaving a trace. When Delano first discovered the child, he suspected that he was the future warrior, or at the very least, he was somehow connected to him. Delano had originally planned to murder the child, but when he got a good look at him, he couldn't bring himself to do it. Hayden reminded him of his own son, Dryden, who had gone missing prior to that moment. Because of Hayden's striking resemblance to Dryden, Delano decided that he wanted to take him and keep him. He came to the child and hypnotized him, and then he took him to his home and put him into a cell in his dungeon. Delano didn't plan to keep him there permanently. He wanted the boy to get used to being there. He also wanted to cause the boy to forget his family and see him as his father.

Delano would go into the cell and spend time with the boy because he wanted him to bond with him. Hayden was somewhat confused because he didn't know how he had gotten there. He also found himself forgetting things from his past and members of his family. The child wasn't sure whether he could trust Delano, since things became more of a blur to him.

As time went on, Delano found himself thinking about Hayden's brother. Even though he saw him as weak, he admired him because of his uniqueness and, like many others, even he saw it as a thing of beauty. Delano decided that he wanted to take him so that he could keep him as his son, just as he did his brother, and he left his home to search for him. He never found him, There was no trace of him anywhere. Delano became disappointed, and he suspected that something bad had happened to the child. With that, he returned to his home.

Because the child was gone, and he had captured Hayden, he felt that he had won. Not only did he prevent the future warrior from coming against him, but he also gained a son. He looked forward to the day when Hayden would see him as his father, and he was also happy that he had a child to love and take care of.

Chapter 2

Endymion refused to give up on the hope of the possibility of finding the one who was responsible for the disappearances so that he could bring him to justice and put an end to his evil deeds. He decided to continue his search in hopes of bringing his loved ones home safely. Liam was planning to go with him because he wanted to help. He also had an idea of what it was that they were up against, even though the perpetrator was difficult to locate.

Endymion assigned several of his guards to watch over everyone while he was gone. While many didn't understand

and they thought he was trying to hold them captive, they didn't know his true motive, which was actually to protect them. He also wanted his wife and children to remain safe while he was away as he continued his search to find the missing people and the one who was responsible for their disappearances.

Before Endymion and Liam left, Endymion hugged each of his sons, whose names were Devon and Dalton, and gave them each a kiss.

"I love you, father." Devon said.

"I love you too, son." Endymion said.

Then Dalton started to cry.

"I wish you didn't have to go." he said.

"I know, son, but there are things that I must do, but I will return." Endymion said.

"I'll miss you." Dalton said.

"I already miss you." Devon said.

"I know, my sons. I'll miss you both as well." Endymion said.

He gave them both another hug. Then he hugged his wife, Lilly, tightly.

"Please, be careful." Lilly said.

"I'll try, my love. I want you to stay safe. There will be guards around to keep an eye on things while I'm away. There will also be some who will watch over you and the children." Endymion said.

He then gave Lilly a kiss.

"Don't open the door for anyone. It's not that I'm trying to be overbearing. It's just that I want to keep you safe. Also, I don't trust Levi and I don't want him near you." Endymion said.

"Would he really mistreat a woman?" Liam asked.

"Because she's my wife, he may. Also, he bullies children. I don't want him anywhere near my sons. He's already tormented my grandson, and he even tried to murder him, so I'd put nothing past him." Endymion said.

"I'm really sorry." Liam said.

"Why are you sorry? You have no control over his actions." Endymion said.

"It's because of who he is. It sickens me that he would act that way toward an innocent child."

"You don't need to apologize for him. He'll have to answer for his actions someday. In the meantime, we should probably go." Endymion said.

He then looked at Lilly before he gave her a kiss. Then he hugged her tightly.

"I'll miss you while I'm gone." Endymion said.

"I'll miss you too." Lilly said.

Endymion and Liam then left to continue their mission to stop the horrible things that had been happening.

Chapter 3

Meanwhile, in his underground home, Delano sat alone as he thought about how nice it would be to have someone to spend the rest of his life with. He had been alone for several years, and he missed having a woman in his life. He also wanted to find a mother for the child who remained in his dungeon. Delano thought that it was the perfect time to start over. Delano went to the room where he kept the child. He looked at him for a moment before he sat down beside him. The child remained silent as he looked at Delano nervously.

"I plan to go away for a bit, but I will return shortly. Do you need anything?" Delano said.

The boy didn't respond.

"Very well. As I said, I will return shortly." Delano said.

He stood up, and then he vanished from his home. As he looked around, he suddenly remembered the woman who had captured his attention several years ago. He decided that if there was anyone that he wanted to start a family with, she was the one. With that, he teleported to the place where he had seen her.

Delano wasted no time. To avoid being seen, he teleported into the house right away. He glanced around before he went to where he could be hidden. Delano remained silent as he watched for the one who he was determined to make his wife. He tried to be patient as he waited, even though he saw no sign of her.

As time went on, Delano became frustrated because he felt that he was wasting his time. He was about to leave when, suddenly, she entered the room. Delano watched her closely as she put clothes and other things away. He wanted to approach her, but then he thought about how everyone saw him as a monster. Delano suddenly feared the possibility of her also thinking that he was a monster. He decided it was best if he just left since he felt that he had no chance of winning her over.

Chapter 4

Delano went back to his home and right away he started to pace the floor. Then he stopped for a moment before he teleported to the dungeon. He looked right at Conner before he pointed at him.

"You! Come!" Delano said.

Without hesitation, Conner made his way over to him.

"Is there something wrong?" Conner asked.

"I need someone to talk to. I suppose that you'll do." Delano said.

He then took Conner and teleported to his room.

"Sit down." Delano said.

Conner sat down and watched Delano as he paced the floor.

"Perhaps you should sit down." Conner said.

"Don't tell me what to do!" Delano said.

"It was just a suggestion. It's obvious that you have something on your mind that's bothering you." Conner said.

Delano stopped pacing the floor, and then he glanced at Conner before he sat down.

"Talk to me." Conner said.

"It's been several years since Lela passed away. I miss having a family. I managed to capture the child that looks like my son, but I long for a woman to share my life with. Also, I feel that it would be beneficial if the child had a mother to take care of him."

"So go find one."

"Would you let me finish!" Delano said.

"Right."

"As I was saying, I miss having someone in my life. Since I've captured the child, and in doing so, I have defeated my future enemy, I've decided that the time has come for me to find someone to spend the rest of my life with. As I left my home, I remembered the beautiful woman that had caught my attention years ago."

"Why didn't you go to her if you feel that the time has come for you to find someone?" Conner asked.

"I did, and I saw her. She was as beautiful as the last time that I saw her."

"Then, what's the trouble?" Conner asked.

"I was going to approach her, but I stopped myself."

"Why?"

"Because I feared the possibility of her thinking that I was a monster, so I left."

"Why would you have that fear? You have a lot to offer."

"She may not see it that way. Many do see me as a monster." Delano said.

"Obviously the one who you were with before didn't see you as a monster, seeing as she was your wife, and you had children with her. How did you win her over?"

"It was very different with Lela. We met at a very early age. We were just small children when we first met."

"How young were you?"

"I was five."

"You were young." Conner said.,

"She found me alone, and she befriended me right away. We became best friends. As time went on, our feelings grew, and we fell in love. There will never be another like her."

"I'm very sorry."

"Lela can never be replaced. Nevertheless, it's been several years since she departed, and now I want the beautiful creature who has captured my attention to be my wife."

"Then you must pursue her."

"That's easier said than done." Delano said.

"You can't give up, not if you want her and a family with her. Also, it is true that the child should have a mother."

"I do want her and I want more children. I've always wanted a big family. I would've had that, had it not been taken away from me in the first place."

"Then you must win her over. Leave her gifts and other things that would make her happy. I truly believe that you have what it takes to make her fall in love with you."

"I'm not so sure about that."

"If all else fails, you could always hypnotize her."

"No. I want her to fall in love with me on her own."

"Then you know what you must do."

"I'm not even sure about where to begin."

"You'll figure it out. I believe in you."

"I almost wish that meant something to me. Nonetheless, it would mean a lot to me if she'd fall in love with me and would want to spend her life with me. It would make me happy to have her here with me." Delano said.

"Then go to her and don't give up until you win her over."

Chapter 5

The following day, Delano decided to go back to where he saw the woman who he wanted to be a part of his life. Before he went back, he decided to pick a bouquet of red flowers because red was his favorite color. After he picked the bouquet, he went to the house, where the woman was. He quickly placed them where he hoped she would see them, and then he hid. Delano remained quiet as he waited patiently in his hiding spot. He hoped that she would soon enter the room, so she would see the gift that he had left for her.

Time passed, and she didn't come into the room. Delano found himself becoming frustrated and impatient. Once again, he thought that he was wasting his time. Then suddenly, she entered the room. She was bewildered as she noticed the bouquet of beautiful flowers. She made her way over to them, and then she picked them up and looked at them for a moment before she left the room with them. Delano wasn't sure what to think at that moment. He wasn't sure whether she liked the flowers that he had left for her. Delano sighed, and then he left and headed back to his home.

Chapter 6

After Delano had returned to his home, he started to pace the floor. As he walked back and forth across the room, he began to wonder about whether he was wasting his time. He truly wanted to believe that he had a chance to win the woman's heart, but he believed that his chances were slim due to how most people viewed him. As Delano continued to doubt the possibility of finding love again, he became frustrated. He started to wonder about whether he should give up. Then he teleported to the dungeon.

"Oh, great, he's back." Damien said.

Delano ignored him as he made his way over to Conner.

"Is everything alright?" Conner asked.

"I need someone to talk to." Delano said.

Conner stood up, and then he looked right at him. Then he and Delano vanished. Conner sat down while Delano started to pace the floor.

"Can you please sit down?" Conner asked.

"No."

"I think that you need to relax." Conner said.

Delano sighed.

"Very well." he said.

He then sat down.

"Talk to me." Conner said.

"I feel like I'm wasting my time."

"Talking is never a waste of time."

"No, I'm not talking about that. I'm talking about me pursuing that woman."

"Why?"

"Look at me. Who is either of us kidding? She'd never look twice at me. More than likely, she'll try to run away from me the second she does see me."

"Why?"

"Let's face it. Almost everyone who has seen me has called me a monster. Even Lela has called me a monster."

"I thought that she loved you."

"She did. She laid down her life for me. She knew that others saw me as a monster, but she didn't care. She still loved me. Lela said that I was beautiful and that I was her monster. Although I hate being referred to as a monster, I loved the fact that she called me hers in spite of it."

"What makes you think that this woman wouldn't find you attractive? You fit the description of what most women want."

"As nice as that all sounds, I find that hard to believe."

"But it's true." Conner said.

"I doubt it."

"Listen to me, women like tall, dark, and handsome, and that's you."

"What's the point?"

"I don't want you to give up. You want a wife and a chance to start over and have a family."

"I do want that, and now since I've succeeded at eliminating my future enemy, I would like to find a wife to settle down with and I want to start a family before I establish my kingdom."

"Then don't give up. You have so much to offer, not to mention, practically your entire life ahead of you. Show her what you have to offer. I'm sure that you'll have her eating out of the palm of your hand if you'd just give it time. You must be patient."

"I'm not a patient man." Delano said.

"Unfortunately, there are things that you cannot rush."

"I suppose you're right."

"I believe in you. I truly believe that you will find someone. Who knows?

Maybe you'll have all the women swooning over you."

"Perhaps in my dreams."

"If all else fails…"

"I'm not going to hypnotize her. I want a woman to fall in love with me on her own. I shouldn't have to coerce her into it. That's not love at all."

"But you can't just give up, not if it's what you want."

"It is what I want."

"Then go get her."

"I suppose I could keep trying. I really don't have anything to lose, but I have much to gain by not giving up, especially if I do win her over." Delano said.

"That's true, and even if she isn't the one, I'm sure that there are plenty more out there who would find you desirable."

"Desirable?"

"Why not?" Conner asked.

"In that case, I must go back. I won't give up until I get what I want."

Chapter 7

Delano decided to go back to where the woman lived. Before he went back, he decided to gather rubies and other things that he would need because he wanted to make a necklace for the woman that he wanted to spend his life with. He wasted no time, and he started on it right away. Delano worked on it diligently until he had gotten it completed. When he had finished it, he decided to go to the dungeon to ask Conner what he thought about it.

"Is everything alright?" Conner asked.

"I hope so. I'm going to go back to the woman's home, and I made something for her. I hope that she will like it." Delano said.

He then showed Conner the necklace that he had made.

"So, what do you think? Do you think she'll like it? As I said, I made it myself, and I put a lot of thought and hard work into it." Delano said.

"I'm sure that any woman would love it. It's beautiful. I can see that you have put a lot of work into it."

"I have. I truly hope that she'll like it."

"There's only one way you'll find out. Go to her and give it to her."

"Right. I suppose I'll be on my way now." Delano said.

He vanished from the dungeon to go back to where the woman was, so he

could give her the gift that he had made
for her.

Chapter 8

When Delano arrived, he glanced around before he placed the necklace where the woman would see it. Then he went to his hiding spot, so he wouldn't end up being discovered. He still wasn't sure whether the time was right for him to reveal himself to her. Delano still feared the possibility of her fearing him and thinking that he was a monster, so he decided that it was best for him to remain hidden.

As Delano waited, he tried to remain patient, even though it was difficult for him. He wanted to witness the moment when the woman would enter the room and discover the necklace that he had left for her.

Unfortunately, as time went on, Delano started to lose his patience as he continued to wait in his hiding spot for the woman to enter the room. He grew tired of waiting, and he was about to leave when she entered the room. As she started to put things away, she noticed the necklace on the dresser, and she picked it up. Then she looked at it for a moment before she sat down and studied it closely. Delano remained quiet as he watched her. He wanted to come out from his hiding spot and talk to her, but he was afraid to. He began to wonder if the right moment would ever come when he would have enough courage to approach her. Then the woman got up and left the room. Delano became disappointed since she was no longer in the room. He decided to leave and go back to his home.

Chapter 9

After Delano returned to his home, he started to pace the floor, and then he stopped for a moment as he started to think. Then he vanished from his living room and ended up in the cell where he was keeping Hayden. The child became startled as he noticed him standing in the room looking right at him.

"Hello, my child." Delano said.

Hayden said nothing as he kept his eyes on Delano, who then sat down beside him.

"I'm sorry that I haven't been spending as much time with you these days. I was on a very important mission." Delano said.

Hayden didn't respond.

"How have you been feeling?" Delano asked.

Hayden didn't answer.

"You don't need to be afraid of me. I have no intention of hurting you. I want to take care of you. That's why I brought you here." Delano said.

He fought back tears as he looked into Hayden's eyes.

"The truth is, you remind me of someone who meant a lot to me, someone whom I loved very much." Delano said.

His eyes filled with tears as he kept his eyes on the child, who had a sad expression on his face. Then he gave Delano a hug. Delano smiled as he hugged the child, and then he spoke to him.

"Once my mission is completed, I'll be able to spend more time with you. We will be a family. I'm sorry that I was unable to find your brother. I fear that the worst may have happened to him. Had I known, I would've taken him the first time I saw him. I promise you that you will have many brothers to play with and a mother who will care for you. We will be a family and have a new beginning, you will see."

Chapter 10

Delano made up his mind to go back to where the woman lived. He felt that the time had come to pursue her and make her his wife. With that, he prepared himself. Delano wanted to look his best for the occasion. He was all dressed in black, as he always was, and he wore a black leather button-down shirt. He wanted to do everything he could to impress her since they would be meeting for the first time.

Before Delano went to the woman's home, he gathered food and water for Hayden. He wanted to make sure he had plenty to eat while he was away. Afterward, Delano left his home. Before he went to the woman's home, he decided to get a red long stem rose because he wanted to make the occasion as special as possible. He wanted to do everything possible to win her over. Delano was a bit nervous about approaching her, mainly because he was afraid of the possibility of her becoming afraid of him. He wasn't about to give up on his chance at happiness. Delano was determined to make her his wife so that he could settle down with her and start a family.

Chapter 11

One day, Lilly was busy touching up the house when suddenly, she caught a glimpse of something. When she looked again, she saw nothing there. Lilly continued to clean the house when she heard something. She glanced around, but she still saw nothing.

Lilly decided to go upstairs to make sure there was nothing suspicious. She went into her room and looked around, but she saw nothing. Then she turned and as she glanced at the doorway of the room, she saw someone standing there looking right at her as he held a red long-stemmed rose. Tension built up inside her as she kept her eyes on the stranger who stood there as he continued to look at her.

"Who...who are you? How did you get here?" Lilly asked.

The stranger smelled the rose that he was holding as he kept his eyes on her. She took a step back as he entered the room.

"Rather than asking how I got here, why not ask why I came?" he said.

"Why are you here?"

"Because you've taken something from me."

"I don't know what you're talking about." Lilly said.

"I've come because you've stolen my heart. You captured my attention years ago."

"No."

"I've waited for so long for the right moment to approach you. For a while, I was afraid and the time didn't seem right. Now, the moment has come."

"No."

"Yes, it's true. I've been lonely for so long. I miss the company of a beautiful woman. I long for it, and my heart yearns for you."

As Lilly looked into the stranger's eyes, her heart sank and chills went through her spine as she began to tremble.

"No. It can't be." Lilly said.

She started to back away from the stranger, who kept his eyes on her as he moved toward her.

"Is there something wrong, my dear?" he asked.

"It's you."

"Who?" he asked.

Lilly trembled as she looked into his eyes.

"Del." she said.

"I love how it sounds when you say my name." he said.

He continued to move toward her as he kept his eyes on her.

"Say it again." he said.

Lilly continued to back away, even as he continued to move toward her. As he got closer, Lilly suddenly seemed perplexed as she looked at him.

"You seem troubled about something." Delano said.

"Who are you?"

"I thought you knew who I was, after all, you said my name."

"But where did you come from?"

"Why do you ask?" Delano asked.

"Are you from this area?"

"No. Why do you ask?"

"You look a lot like my husband." Lilly said.

"Your husband? I could be your husband." Delano said.

When he approached Lilly, he looked into her eyes for a moment, and then he tried to kiss her, but she looked away, and he ended up kissing her cheek.

"I understand. This is all so sudden. Perhaps you need time to get to know me." Delano said.

"Get to know you? I'm married."

"If you think that will stop me, then you're only kidding yourself."

"I think you should go."

"Actually, I was thinking about staying. I may even make this my second home. I must say that this place is rather impressive." Delano said.

Lilly did not want him to stay. She was terrified of him, especially after all that she had heard about him. The one person who her husband had left to search for had managed to show up, and she began to worry about what would happen next. She wished for Delano to leave, but then she thought for a moment. Lilly started to wonder if she could use Delano being there to her advantage. She thought that if she could keep him there until Endymion and Liam would return, they would finally have the chance to defeat him.

"You know, I've been thinking, and you're absolutely right. I think it would be nice if you would stay here. Maybe we could eventually take some time to get to know one another." Lilly said.

"I like the way that sounds, and I knew that you would come around to my way of thinking. I truly believe that if you give me a chance, I could make you happy. You wouldn't be disappointed." Delano said.

He then stole a kiss from Lilly.

"I really do want to get to know you. I want us to be comfortable with one another. Since you've welcomed me into your home, I feel that we can do that now, and the sooner, the better." Delano said.

As much as Lilly hated the idea of spending time with him, she felt that it could've been a chance to finally stop Delano and put an end to all the destruction that he had been causing.

Chapter 12

As much as Lilly hated the idea of Delano staying in her home with her, she wanted even more for him to be stopped. The thought of being alone with him terrified her, but she knew that she had to remain calm, and she couldn't let him know that he made her uncomfortable. She was also fearful about how far he would try to go with her and what he would do if she would resist him. With that, she decided that it was best to just continue with what she was doing before she discovered him in her home. Lilly tried to ignore him as she kept busy, but it did no good. He made it obvious that he wanted her to acknowledge the fact that he was there, and that he didn't like being ignored. He was determined to get her attention, so he snuck his way over to her, and then he put his arms around her before he spoke into her ear.

"I think you should take a break." he said.

"I need to get this done."

"Perhaps I could help you."

"I can handle it."

"I do believe that it would be much better if I helped you. Don't you think so? The way I see it, the sooner we get the work done, the more time we'd have to spend together so that we can get to know one another. I really want to get to know you." Delano said.

The thought of it sent chills down Lilly's spine. The last thing she wanted was to get to know him. She wanted to run away from him, but she had a feeling that her chances of escaping would be slim. She wanted the nightmare to be over, but she feared that it had only begun. Lilly also knew that more than likely it would do no good to argue with him, and she was afraid to. Remembering the things that she heard about him, she feared him because she knew that he could kill her at any time if he wanted to.

Lilly couldn't wait for Endymion and Liam to return, but as she thought about it, she began to worry about the possibility of Delano killing them. She wanted her husband to take Delano down, but at the same time, she couldn't bear the thought of him getting killed. As she continued to think about it, she started to think that it would be better if Endymion would not return because she knew how dangerous Delano was. She felt threatened by his presence and the last thing she wanted was for her husband to return, only to meet his demise, especially knowing that all it would take was just one bite.

Chapter 13

After finishing the work that needed to be done, Delano took Lilly by the hand, and he took her into the living room where they both sat down. The two of them were quiet as they sat on the sofa. Delano kept his eyes on Lilly, who tried to avoid eye contact with him. Then he moved closer to her before he gave her a kiss on the cheek.

"Are you alright, my dear? You seem tense." he said.

"I just need to relax."

"I do agree. It would make things a bit easier. Perhaps I could help you to become more relaxed."

"No, I'm fine."

"I thought we were going to take time to get to know one another. I feel like we're not off to a good start." Delano said.

"What do you mean? I said that I needed to relax and that's what I'm doing."

"I think that we could be more relaxed upstairs in your room."

"I don't feel like going to my room."

"Perhaps later on." Delano said.

Lilly said nothing as she looked at Delano, who stole a kiss from her.

"I must say that I like what I see so far." Delano said.

Lilly said nothing as she looked at him nervously.

"I apologize if it seems that I'm moving too quickly. I've been a lonely man for several years. I long to have a family. The thing is, I'm not a patient man. I know exactly what I want, and what I want is for you to be my wife and the mother of my children." Delano said

"He then touched the side of her face as he looked into her eyes.

"We could have a beautiful thing together. It would be like a beautiful flower, much like the ones I had left for you. With time and the proper care, it could blossom into something magnificent. Don't you think so?" Delano said.

Lilly didn't respond.

"I understand that this all seems sudden, and   things are happening rather quickly. The truth is, neither of us are getting any younger. I think it's soon time to think about starting a family. I have no doubt that it would be wonderful. We make an elegant couple and our children would be beautiful." Delano said.

Lilly said nothing.

"I understand. The very thought of it has left you speechless. It's okay. I'm not upset because I realize that it's probably a shock to you. It's probably like a dream for you. I know it's a dream come true for me." Delano said.

It was more like a horrible nightmare for Lilly, and she wondered if it would ever come to an end.

Chapter 14

Lilly found it difficult to relax since Delano refused to leave her alone. She got up from where she was sitting and without saying a word, she headed upstairs to her room. Delano watched silently as she walked away. When Lilly got to the top of the stairs, she glanced back before she headed to her room. As she entered the room, she found Delano on the bed with his shirt partially unbuttoned, and he was looking right at her. Lilly turned and was about to leave when Delano appeared in front of her, and then he took hold of her arm.

"Where do you think you're going?" Delano asked.

Lilly didn't respond as she looked at him nervously.

"I'm starting to feel like you're toying with me. If I were you, I wouldn't do that." Delano said.

"But I didn't do anything."

"Then why did you try to leave the room? Is it because of me?"

"I told you that I wanted to relax, but you're not letting me relax."

"I'm not doing anything to prevent you from relaxing. I was under the impression that we were going to spend time together, but I feel like you're trying to avoid me." Delano said.

Lilly said nothing as she looked at him nervously.

"Do I make you uncomfortable? Do you fear me so much that you can't stand to be around me?" Delano asked.

"I can't do this."

"Why not?" Delano asked.

Lilly didn't respond.

"I knew it. I figured this would happen." Delano said.

"What are you talking about?"

"I know that you see me as a monster. I can tell. It's the whole reason I was reluctant to reveal myself to you in the first place."

"I never said that you were a monster."

"Who are you kidding? It's okay for those purple men to roam the neighborhood, and they're not seen as monsters. They may actually even be seen as human. Meanwhile, people take one look at me, and they see me as a creature of the night that needs to be destroyed."

"I can clearly see that you are human."

"I am quite human, although many seem to think otherwise. Everyone has always seen me as a monster, but you see, I'm not so different from anyone else. I have wants and needs, just as other people do. Believe it or not, even so-called monsters like me need to be loved. Nobody ever stops and thinks about the fact that I require the same things as everyone else in order to survive. No one considers the fact that I actually have feelings. I have a heart that beats, and it can be broken. I hunger and I thirst, and I breathe air, just as you do. To you, my eyes may be seen as scary, but you couldn't count the number of tears that I've cried. The thing is, I am capable of love. I could show you how capable I truly am if only you would let me." Delano said.

He then took hold of Lilly's hands as he looked into her eyes. He wouldn't take his eyes off of her, even as he kissed her hands.

"Please, give me a chance. Let me show you how loving I can be." Delano said.

At first, Lilly hesitated to respond. Delano sighed as he shook his head with an unhappy expression on his face.

"I knew it." he said.

"Wait. I'll give you a chance under one condition."

"What would that be?"

"Please, just slow down. You're moving much too quickly." Lilly said.

Delano sighed, and then he responded.

"Very well, but I don't want to take it too slow. I was hoping that we could soon move forward in our relationship with a bright future ahead of us. As I said before, neither of us are getting any younger, and I want to start a family with you."

Chapter 15

Lilly was relieved that Delano had agreed to slow down. She hoped that she would be able to find peace, even while being stuck as a prisoner in her own home with Delano. She was so afraid that he would discover her sons. Lilly didn't want him anywhere near them, and she hoped that they would remain hidden from him, especially after what had happened to so many people in the community. A part of her wished that Endymion and Liam would return so that the nightmare would come to an end, even though she was afraid that something terrible would happen.

Lilly was going to check on her sons when Delano stopped her.

"What are you doing?" Delano asked.

Lilly didn't respond.

"Why don't we sit down?" Delano asked.

"I have something that I need to do."

"It can wait." Delano said.

Lilly sighed, and then she and Delano walked over to the sofa and sat down. Delano glanced at her before he took hold of Lilly's hand. Chills ran down her spine as she felt his soft lips pressed against her hand. Then Delano tried to kiss her, but she turned her face.

"I wish you wouldn't do that." Delano said.

"What have I done to upset you this time?"

"You turned your face whenever I tried to give you a kiss." Delano said.

He had a sad expression on his face as he looked into her eyes.

"Why must you do that? I mean you no harm. I just want to be loved." Delano said.

With a sad expression still on his face, Delano took Lilly's hand and put it against his face.

"Why won't you love me? Do you think that I am ugly?" Delano asked.

Lilly looked away.

"You think that I'm a monster." Delano said.

"I never said that."

"Then why did you look away?"

"Please, don't be upset."

"Then give me what I want." Delano said.

Lilly frowned as she looked at Delano, who stole a kiss from her. Then he moved closer to her as he kept his eyes on her. He closed his eyes as he gave her another kiss before he rested against her.

"I thought you said that you were going to slow down." Lilly said.

Delano sat up, and then he looked at her sternly.

"I have." he said.

"Have you?"

"It was just a kiss."

"What makes you think that I was ready for a kiss?"

"Look, I told you that I'm not a patient man. I'm thirty-three years old, and I'm not getting any younger."

"You're thirty-three?"

"Yes."

"Why, you're just a baby." Lilly said.

"A baby? Why don't you let this baby show you what he's capable of."

"Are you upset?"

"I don't particularly like being referred to as an infant. I'm a grown man, and furthermore, I've been on my own taking care of myself even at a very early age. I'm not a baby. I'm probably more grown up than most of the people in this neighborhood." Delano said.

"I'm sorry. I didn't mean to upset you. It's just that you're even younger than my husband, and he's a few years younger than me."

"So? Did you actually think that it would bother me? Think again. I couldn't care less."

"Maybe I'm not sure how I feel about it."

"You don't seem to have a problem with your husband being younger than you."

"That's because he's just a few years younger than me. You, on the other hand, are a bit more than just a few years younger."

"Are you sure that you're not telling me a lie? You don't look that much older than me. I feel like you're just trying to make up an excuse to not be with me."

"No, it's true."

"In case you didn't know, I still don't care. I still want you as my wife. Correct me if I'm wrong, but I recall you mentioning that I resemble your husband. If that's the case, he can't be that much older than me. Also, you can pretend that I'm him if that makes it easier for you. As for your husband, I haven't yet decided what to do with him yet. I'll either kill him or make him my slave. If he was the one who built this beautiful house, perhaps I could spare his life and make use of him."

"You're still upset."

"Yes. You told me that you would give me a chance, but I feel like you're not doing that. Instead, you're pointing out my age and acting as though it's a problem." Delano said.

He then sighed before he rested against Lilly.

"Please, don't use my age as an excuse to not be with me. I'm not a child, I'm a man who has wants and needs. I want a family and I need you to cooperate with me. You told me that you would give me a chance." Delano said.

"And you told me that you would slow down."

"I did slow down. I see nothing wrong with me wanting a kiss." Delano said.

"Very well. I'll overlook your age, and I'll give you a chance, but you need to slow down." Lilly said.

Delano sat up, looked at Lilly, and then he gave her a kiss before he rested against her again.

"Very well. I will slow down, however, you can't expect me to not kiss you, because I want what's mine, and if I want to give you a kiss, you're just going to have to accept it. The way I see it, we should be able to meet halfway. I'll slow down, but in turn, you will not turn your face when I want to kiss you. Do I make myself clear?" Delano said.

"Yes."

"Good." Delano said.

He sat up and looked into Lilly's eyes before he closed his eyes and kissed her. Then he laid down, and he sighed as he rested against her.

Chapter 16

As time went on, Delano grew even more impatient, and he decided to confront Lilly about it.

"I need to have a word with you." Delano said.

"What's the matter?" Lilly asked.

"I'm tired of taking things slow. I told you before that I'm not a patient man. I think it's about time we move forward in our relationship."

"I'm not ready to move forward yet."

"Why not?" Delano asked.

He shook his head as he looked at her sternly.

"It's because of him. Isn't it?" Delano said.

Lilly didn't respond.

"Have you been toying with me?" Delano asked.

"No."

"You better cooperate with me, unless you want him to die." Delano said.

"No, please don't."

"Why must we take things so slow?"

"I'm sorry that you feel that we're taking things too slowly. I just don't feel comfortable with where I feel this is going. I'm not ready for what it is that you're wanting to do."

"When will you be comfortable with it? How long will it take until you are ready?"

"I thought that you said that you wanted us to get to know each other."

"What did you think I meant whenever I said that?"

"I had a feeling that's what you meant, but I'm not ready for that."

"Well, I am, in fact, I'll never stop being ready. I'm tired of waiting. I want a family with lots and lots of children." Delano said.

Lilly said nothing as she looked into Delano's eyes. She could see that he was frustrated, but she didn't want to give in. She thought for a moment about how she hoped that her husband would soon return. Lilly realized that she had to do something to try to calm Delano down.

"Can't I have just a little more time?" she asked.

"How much time do you need?"

"If you truly loved me, you wouldn't even ask."

"If you loved me, you'd quit playing these games." Delano said.

"Why must you be so angry?"

"You don't know what it feels like to go through the things I went through. I've had everything taken from me. My entire life was ruined. I'm tired of being alone and unloved. I want to be able to start over."

"Please, just give me a little more time. I promise that whenever I'm ready, I'll give you what you want."

"Prove it." Delano said.

"What?"

"I'm not fully convinced. I feel like you just keep playing mind games, toying with my affections. I don't like that very much. If your man is the problem, I'll make sure to take care of the problem. He won't be an issue whenever I'm finished."

"What do you want me to do?"

"Give me a kiss."

"A kiss?"

"Yes." Delano said.

Lilly hesitated for a moment before she gave him a kiss on the cheek.

"Nice try, but what I want is a kiss on the lips." Delano said.

Tension rose inside Lilly as she looked at Delano, who was clearly waiting to see if she would kiss him. She really didn't want to do it, but at the same time, she didn't want Delano to murder Endymion. Lilly closed her eyes, and then she gave Delano a kiss. Delano put his arms around her as he kissed her. Then he looked into her eyes for a moment before he hugged her tightly as he spoke.

"Perhaps I could give you a little more time, but only a few days. That should be plenty of time for you to become comfortable enough to give me what I want. I promise to make you happy. Together we will have a beautiful family. I will never disappoint you."

Chapter 17

Early the next morning, Lilly decided that she was going to try to get help. She didn't want to be stuck with Delano any longer, so she decided to do something about it. Lilly also didn't want anything to happen to Endymion, so she became desperate. She was even willing to find Kurtis, even though she never saw him. She hoped that he would be willing to help her if she asked him. Without hesitation, she got up and left the room. Before she left, she went into her sons' room for a moment.

"I have to go out for a moment. I want the two of you to remain hidden. I'll be back shortly." Lilly said.

"Okay, mother." Devon said.

"Stay safe." Lilly said.

"I'm scared, mother." Dalton said.

"I know, but hopefully soon, it'll be over." Lilly said.

"I wish father would come home soon." Dalton said.

"I know, but I'm going to go and get some help. In the meantime, hide, and don't let him find you." Lilly said.

She then gave them each a kiss on their foreheads before she left the room. Lilly went down the stairs and rushed toward the door. She thought for sure that she would be able to get help, but then, Delano appeared in front of the door.

"You seem to be in a hurry." Delano said.

Lilly took a step back as she looked at Delano.

"Where are you going?" he asked.

Lilly didn't respond.

"You were trying to escape, weren't you." Delano said.

Lily turned and ran as she headed toward another door. Unfortunately, it did no good because Delano appeared in front of the door.

"You will find that it'll do no good to try to escape. I've gotten used to this place, so I'm aware of every exit that's in this place." Delano said.

Lilly took a step back before she turned and ran. She rushed up the stairs and into her room. She ran toward the window as she hoped that she would be able to escape. Then Delano appeared in the room. He looked at her angrily as she tried to get the window open. Delano moved toward her and when he approached her, he took hold of her.

"You'll never escape me." Delano said.

"Please, let me go."

"No. I knew it. You had no intention of settling down with me. That infuriates me, therefore, I'm going to give you two choices. Either you give me what I want, or you will face the consequences." Delano said.

Lilly didn't respond as she tried to get away from him.

"Very well, then have it your way." Delano said.

He took her to the bed, and then he forced her down onto it. He pinned her down before he started kissing her.

"If you are wise, you won't give me any trouble." Delano said.

Lilly continued to try to escape him. Then Delano spoke softly into her ear.

"I see that you don't want to cooperate with me. That makes me unhappy, and it's really too bad that it had to come to this. I thought that we could've had a beautiful thing, but I can see that it just was never meant to be." Delano said.

He started kissing her again before he sank his teeth into her, even as she continued to try to get away from him. It was moments later when she stopped struggling, and she became motionless. Delano gave her one last kiss, and then he stood up, and he looked at Lilly for a moment before he left the room. He was about to leave when he heard something coming from another room. He made his way to the room where the sound was coming from, which was the boys' room. Delano thought for a moment before he teleported into the room. He glanced around the room, and then he walked over to the closet and opened the door. There he discovered the two boys, who looked at him nervously.

"What do we have here? She had children?" Delano said.

The two boys started to tremble as they both looked at him.

"I think I'm going to keep the two of you because you both look like my sons. I have a room where I could put you, where you'll be right at home. There's another little boy there who's about your age. The two of you can be his brothers." Delano said.

The two boys started to cry as they looked at Delano, who then caused them both to fall asleep. Then he took them, and he vanished, taking them both with him.

Chapter 18

It was later that day when Endymion and Liam returned. Endymion could sense right away that there was something wrong.

"Lilly?" he said.

He and Liam looked at one another before they started to search the house. They searched every room before they went up the stairs. As they both approached the bedroom, they were both uneasy. Endymion rushed into the room to see if Lilly was alright. When he realized that she wasn't alive, his heart sank.

"No." he said.

He then noticed the bite on her. He cupped his hands to his face as he broke down and wept. Liam glanced around as he noticed that everything was starting to shake. Endymion got up and searched for his sons, but there was no sign of them anywhere.

"No!" he said.

The thunder crashed as everything continued to shake. As Endymion was about to vanish, Liam took hold of his arm. They ended up at a place where they could be alone. As Liam glanced up at the sky, he noticed the lightning flashing through the sky. The wind picked up and the thunder boomed. Endymion fell to his knees, cupped his hands to his face, and wept bitterly. Liam felt sorrowful for him because he had lost his family.

Meanwhile, the people of the community were outside trying to get the things done that they needed to do when they noticed that the sky became dark. As Kurtis glanced up at the sky, he became concerned for everyone's safety. The wind picked up even more, and Kurtis glanced around before he looked up at the sky again. Then Simon approached him before he also looked up at the sky.

"What's happening?" Simon asked.

"I don't know, but it doesn't look good. We need to get everyone inside." Kurtis said.

He, along with Simon, Aston, Afansi, Steve, and Steven Jr. gathered all the people of the community, and then they were taken to the underground shelter where they would be safe. Steve hated the idea of Levi being there, but he knew that at that moment everyone had to be kept safe.

"What's happening?" Steven Jr. asked.

"I'm really not sure, but for some reason, I sensed a deep heaviness in the atmosphere." Kurtis said.

"Was it like the time when we found the man who was deceased?" Afansi asked.

"No, it was different. It was like an intense feeling of distress." Kurtis said.

"What do you make of it?" Steven Jr. asked.

"I really don't know." Kurtis said.

Steve frowned as he stood there quietly. Then he glanced at Aston, who seemed to be uneasy about something.

As time went on, the storm intensified. Even from the underground shelter, they could hear the storm as it raged on. None of them knew what it was that had caused it.

Chapter 19

Several hours had passed, and the storm had died down. Endymion and Liam went back home, and then Endymion took Lilly and laid her to rest. Liam was with him.

After Endymion had laid the love of his life to rest, he broke down and wept. As his tears fell to the ground, purple crystallized flowers came up from the ground. A tear trickled down Liam's face as he stood there quietly. Endymion then stood up, and he wiped the tears from his face before he looked at Liam, who had tears running down his face as he looked at Endymion. The young man rushed over to Endymion and hugged him as he wept. Then he wiped the tears from his face as he looked at Endymion, who was beside himself with grief.

"Come on, son. Let's go home." Endymion said.

Then two of them vanished from the grave site and went home.

Chapter 20

That night, Aston awakened from a dream. He sensed that something was wrong, so he got up, and then he woke Kurtis up.

"What's wrong?" Kurtis asked.

"I woke up from a bad dream. I get the feeling that something terrible happened. I must know for sure." Aston said.

Kurtis frowned as he looked at Aston, who then woke Steve and Afansi up.

"What's going on?" Afansi asked.

"I feel like something is wrong." Aston said.

Then he, Afansi, Kurtis, and Steve vanished from the underground shelter. Steve was suddenly perturbed as he glanced around.

"I'm really not liking where this is going." Steve said.

Aston glanced around until he spotted a recently dug grave.

"No." he said.

He rushed over to it.

"I knew something was wrong." he said.

"What is it?" Afansi asked.

Tears filled Aston's eyes as he looked at his twin brother.

"It's mother. She's…" Aston said.

At that moment, he broke down and wept.

"I'm so sorry, son." Kurtis said.

"My son never had the chance to meet her. Neither of them did. Hugh will never have the chance to see her." Aston said.

Steve's eyes welled up with tears as he looked at Aston. Tears ran down Kurtis' face as he knelt down and hugged Aston, who broke down and wept. Tears ran down Afansi's face as he stood there quietly. As tears ran down Kurtis' face, red and blue crystallized flowers came up from the ground. Purple ones came up from where Aston's tears fell. Kurtis sighed, and then he stood up and made his way over to Afansi and hugged him.

When they were about to go back to the shelter, Kurtis picked one of the red and blue flowers. Then they went back to the underground shelter. At first, Kurtis was worried because he didn't see Aston, but then he appeared.

"Aston?" Kurtis said.

"Yes?"

"Can you take me outside for a moment? There's something that I need to do." Kurtis said.

"Very well." Aston said.

He teleported Kurtis outside.

"Just wait here for a moment. I won't be long." Kurtis said.

He walked in the direction of the quiet place. As he got closer, he stopped for a moment. He took a deep breath, and then he released it before he continued on. He walked past the tunnel and kept going until he reached Endymion's house. Kurtis quietly walked up the steps and onto the porch. As he looked down, he noticed a purple flower on the porch, and he knew that it was Aston who had put it there. Kurtis then sighed, and he took the red and blue flower that he had in his hand and looked at it for a moment before he placed it down beside the one that Aston had left. Then Kurtis turned and walked away. As he headed back, he spotted Aston, who was slowly walking toward him.

"Let's go back to the shelter." Kurtis said.

The two of them vanished and went back to the underground shelter. Meanwhile, Endymion slowly made his way to the door, and then he opened it. Right away, he spotted the flowers that had been left for him. Endymion glanced in the direction of the neighborhood where he wasn't welcome, and then he picked up the flowers before he went back inside and closed the door. He used his powers to preserve the flowers, so they wouldn't wilt. Then he went upstairs and placed them on the nightstand before he sat down. He

cupped his hands to his face as he
mourned over the loss of the love of his
life.